THE CHILDREN'S CLASSICS Collection

Volume 2

Dados Internacionais de Catalogação na Publicação (CIP) de acordo com ISBD

N458 Nesbit, Edith.
Five children and it / Edith Nesbit. - Jandira, SP : W. Books, 2025.
120 p. ; 12,80cm x 19,80cm - (Classics).

ISBN: 978-65-5294-113-8

1. Literatura inglesa. 2. Clássicos. 3. Aventura. 4. Fantasia. 5. Imaginação. I. Título. II. Série.

2024-2497 CDD 823
CDU 821.111-31

Elaborada por Lucio Feitosa - CRB-8/8803
Índice para catálogo sistemático:
1. Literatura inglesa 823.
2. Literatura inglesa 821.111-31

Text based on the original story by Edith Nesbit,
adapted by Catherine Veitch
Illustrations by Archina Laezza

1st edition in 2025
www.cirandacultural.com.br

Five Children and It

Edith Nesbit

W. Books

Cyril

Oldest child

Anthea

Second oldest child

Robert

Middle child

Jane

Second youngest child

Lamb

The baby

Martha

The children's nursemaid

The sand fairy

(It)

A Psammead

Chapter One

Once upon a time there were five brothers and sisters: Cyril, Anthea, Robert, Jane and the baby of the family, who everyone called Lamb. While their mother visited their sick grandmother and their father was away for work, the children went to stay at the White House for the summer. They were looked after by Martha, their nursemaid, and some other servants.

The White House was deep in the countryside, with no other houses nearby. As soon as they arrived, the children excitedly explored outside. The house was covered in the most sweet-smelling white jasmine flowers and looked like a fairy palace. It stood on the edge of a hill, with a wood behind

it, a chalk quarry on one side, and a gravel pit on the other side. At the bottom of the hill were factories with tall, smoking chimneys, and some homes.

The house was quiet and empty and the children were bored after being there for a week.

'Let's take our spades and dig in the gravel pit,' said Cyril. 'We can pretend it's the seaside.'

Each child carried their own spade, and took it in turns to carry

quarry

A place where materials from the earth are mined.

gravel pit

A place where gravel is dug out of the ground.

Lamb. They called their baby brother Lamb because *baa* was the first word he had spoken.

The gravel pit was very large and looked like a giant's sink. Grass and purple and yellow wild flowers grew around the edges at the top of the pit, and there were piles of gravel everywhere. The children played in these piles. They were careful not to get too close to the edges of the pit, in case they slid down its sides.

At first they built a castle, but castles are no fun when there is no swishing sea to fill up the moat, like there is at the seaside. So instead they began to dig the most enormous hole possible. As the world is round, the children imagined that if they dug deep enough they would reach Australia!

They dug and dug until their hands were sandy, hot and red, and their faces were damp and shiny. Lamb was tired and he lay

asleep in a warm huddle in the middle of the half-finished castle.

As the hole got bigger, the gravel turned to soft, dry sand. Anthea's spade hit something, which moved.

'Something's alive!' screamed Anthea, jumping up.

All the children rushed over to the hole that Anthea had dug.

'It must be a rat,' said Robert. 'Father says you find rats in old pits like this.'

'It may be a snake?' suggested Jane, shuddering.

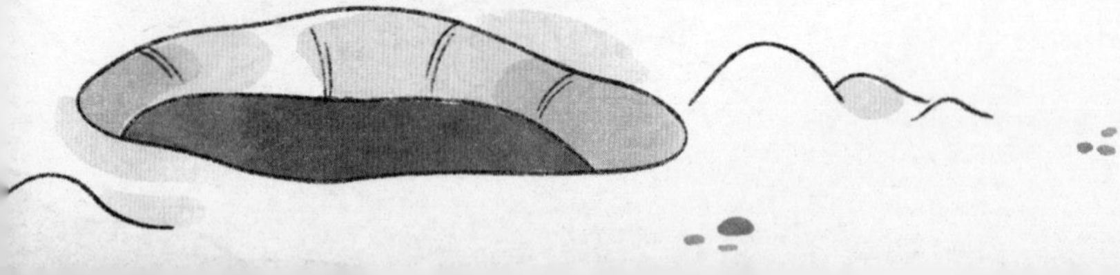

'It's much bigger than a rat,' said Anthea. 'And it's not a snake because it's got feet and fur!'

The children dug carefully so they did not hurt whatever was in the hole. Suddenly, a rough voice in the sand made them all jump.

'Leave me alone,' said the voice.

'I wish you'd come out,' said Anthea bravely.

'If that's your wish,' replied the voice.

Then the sand shook, spun and scattered, and something brown, furry and fat rolled out into the hole. It sat there yawning and

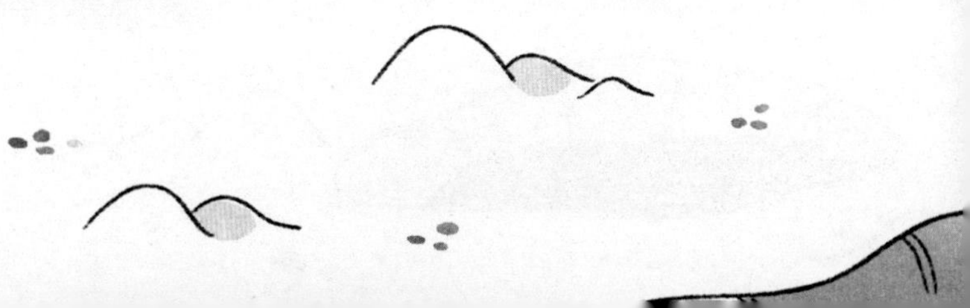

rubbing the ends of its eyes with its hands.

'I must have fallen asleep,' it said, as it stretched.

The children stood round the hole looking at the creature. Its eyes were on long horns like a snail's eyes, and it could move them in and out like telescopes.

It had ears like a bat's ears, and its tubby body was shaped like a spider's and covered with thick, soft fur. Its legs and arms were furry too, and it had hands and feet like a monkey's.

'What are you?' asked Anthea.

'You don't know?' said the creature, surprised. 'I'm a Psammead, of course!'

The creature explained that a Psammead was a type of sand fairy.

'How long have you lived here?' asked Robert.

'Thousands of years,' replied the sand fairy.

'Please tell us everything you can about yourself!' said Jane.

'Thousands of years ago, when people lived in caves, there were many sand fairies. You would go out early in the morning to look for them, and when you found one, you would tell it your wish. But your wish only lasted for that one day, until sunset.'

'Can you give wishes now?' Anthea asked.

'Of course,' the sand fairy replied. 'I gave you your wish just now, when you wished that I would come out.'

The children begged for another wish. The grumpy sand fairy was not too pleased about giving more than one wish in a day, but agreed, just to keep them quiet.

'I wish we were all as beautiful as the countryside,' Anthea said quickly, before the sand fairy changed its mind.

The sand fairy pushed out its long eyes, and puffed out until it was twice as big and twice as furry as before.

Granting wishes was hard work. It stretched out its eyes further than ever and swelled.

‘I hope it won’t hurt itself,’ said Anthea.

‘Or crack its skin,’ said Robert.

Everyone was relieved when the sand fairy suddenly breathed out, and went back to its proper size. It scratched at the sandy gravel with its hands and feet, and then it disappeared. All four children looked at each other. They were now four perfectly beautiful strangers, and did not know each other at first. Then they guessed that Anthea’s wish to the sand fairy to make them all beautiful had come true.

Only Lamb had not changed, as he was still the same beautiful baby that he was before. But because the other four children had changed, Lamb did not know them.

'This is terrible,' said Cyril when he tried to pick up Lamb and Lamb scratched like a cat and bellowed like a bull. 'I can't carry him home, screaming like this!'

After an hour, Lamb calmed down – but only because he was so tired and hungry from all the screaming. He still did not trust the strangers who took it in turns to carry him home.

When they arrived at the house, Martha the nursemaid was waiting anxiously. She snatched Lamb from Jane's arms.

'Thank goodness the baby is back safely. But where are the other children, and who are you all?' Martha asked.

'It's us!' said Robert. 'Only we are now as beautiful as the countryside.'

Martha did not believe Robert and slammed the door. The children had to leave.

'The wish only lasts a day,' said Jane. 'We will look like ourselves again by sunset.'

It was a horrible afternoon. There was no house nearby where the children could beg for a crust of bread or even a glass of water. They were all as beautiful as the countryside, but that is not much help when you are as hungry as a hunter and as thirsty as a sponge. They found a hedge to sit under and waited there for sunset. Eventually their beautiful eyes shut, and they fell asleep.

Anthea woke up first and saw that the sun was setting. It was the end of the day.

'Wake up,' she cried. 'Oh Cyril, you are not so beautiful any more, and nor are any of you,' she added to the others, so they would not feel jealous.

When the children reached home, they were told off by Martha for getting back so late, and she told them about the strange children who had visited earlier.

'They were good-looking but very rude,' Martha said.

And Martha told the children to stay well away from the strange, beautiful children.

Chapter Two

The next morning the children set off for the gravel pit to ask for another wish. They didn't take Lamb with them this time, as Martha had taken him to the town of Rochester to see her cousins. They had made a ring of stones around the place where the sand fairy had disappeared, so they easily found the spot.

The sun was shining brightly and the sky was deep blue, without a cloud in sight.

The children uncovered their spades from the sandy gravel heap where they had buried them and began to dig. It wasn't long before they found the sand fairy.

It sat up and shook the sand out of its fur.

'Do you feel up to giving wishes today?' asked Robert. 'Because we very much want a little, extra wish – as well as the usual one.'

'Give me the little wish first, and I'll see,' said the sand fairy, pushing out its long snail's eyes towards Robert.

'We wish that the servants can't see the gifts you give us,' said Robert.

Robert remembered how angrily Martha had treated them after the last wish.

The sand fairy swelled himself out a bit, breathed out, and then said, 'I've done that for you. It was quite easy. What's your next wish?'

'We wish,' said Robert slowly, 'that

we were rich beyond all our dreams.'

The sand fairy told the children to move away so they wouldn't be buried in gold. Then its skinny arms grew long, and it waved them about so scarily that the children ran as fast as they could towards the road at the edge of the pit.

They turned and looked back, but

had to shut their eyes, because what they saw was too dazzling. The whole of the gravel pit was full to the top with shining gold coins.

Robert stooped down and picked up some coins. Then the rest of the children picked up handfuls of treasure and let it run through their fingers like water.

'Let's fill our pockets and go and buy some things,' said Cyril. 'Don't forget, it only lasts until sunset!'

The children filled their pockets with as many gold coins as they could carry. Then they set off for the nearest village. It was a hot day, the road was dusty and the gold felt heavy in their pockets.

At last they reached an inn on the edge of the village. The children were so hot and thirsty, they agreed to use some of the money to get some lemonade. As Cyril was the oldest, he went in to buy it.

'I had to buy it with my own money, as they laughed at me when I tried to pay with the gold coins,' said Cyril, when he returned with the ice-cold lemonade.

It was Anthea's turn to try to buy something with the gold coins next, as she was the next oldest child. Anthea had more luck. She found an old man called Mr Crispin, who had a horse and cart. Anthea asked Mr Crispin if he would drive them to the nearest big town of Rochester. She was sure there would be lots of things they could buy with their gold in Rochester. Mr Crispin agreed to take the children for one gold coin. It was so much fun riding in a smart cart along the pretty country roads.

However, using the gold coins to buy things in Rochester was not easy. The children went from shop to shop, but none of the shopkeepers wanted their gold. They didn't believe the gold coins were real money and said they looked like fairy money. After a while, the children were tired and hungry, and wanted to go home.

Robert wanted to buy a grand horse and carriage to travel home in. He found Mr Peasemarsh, who had horses and carriages to sell. However, when Robert asked the gentleman if he could buy one,

Mr Peasemarsh laughed at him.

'Who are you kidding? I don't believe you even have two pennies in your pocket!' exclaimed Mr Peasemarsh.

The other children begged Robert to leave, but it was too late. Robert was angry and pulled large handfuls of gold coins from out of his pockets.

'What do you think this is?' Robert asked.

Mr Peasemarsh thought Robert must have stolen the gold coins, so he fetched the police. When a policewoman arrived, she thought the children had stolen the gold coins, too, and led the shocked children away. As they walked around the corner, they bumped into a friendly face … it was Martha, with Lamb!

Martha did not believe what the policewoman or Mr Peasemarsh had accused the children of, even when they made Robert turn out his pockets and show her the gold coins.

'I don't see anything,' she said. 'There isn't any gold there.'

The children were thankful to Martha for sticking up for them.

But then they remembered their wish to the sand fairy that the servants would not be able to see any of the fairy's gifts. Of course, Martha couldn't see the gold! But the children were not free yet, as the policewoman and Mr Peasemarsh *could* see the coins.

It was getting dark by the time they all reached the police station. The policewoman told Robert to turn out his pockets. Robert plunged his hands into his pockets, and he began to laugh, as there were no longer any coins there! He showed the police that his pockets were empty. The other children were ordered to turn out their pockets, too, and they were also empty. The coins had disappeared because the sand fairy's magic ran out at sunset.

'I don't know where they've hidden those coins! They walked in front of me all the way here,' said the puzzled policewoman.

Martha demanded that the police send her and the children home in a grand carriage. Even though the children were not in trouble with the police, they were still in trouble with Martha for going to Rochester on their own.

And so, after a day of being rich beyond their dreams, the children were sent to bed in disgrace yet again.

Chapter Three

The next morning over breakfast, the children talked about the sand fairy and the bad luck they'd had with their wishes.

'We must try to find a wish that works this time,' said Cyril.

Martha caught them at the gate as they were leaving for the pit, and asked them to take Lamb out to play with them.

When they reached the pit, they could not find the sand fairy.

Since the pit was filled with gold yesterday, they hadn't been able to mark the spot with stones. The children looked for a long while, but only found their spades. Searching for sand fairies was tiring work, especially when they took it in turns to carry little Lamb. So they sat down for a rest, and put Lamb on the ground.

Lamb playfully rolled over in the sand, but howled when he got it in his eyes. Luckily, Robert had brought a bottle of water with him.

He tried to rinse the sand out of Lamb's eyes, but that only made Lamb howl louder.

'Oh why didn't Martha look after Lamb? Our lives would be so much easier if she looked after him. I wish everyone wanted Lamb with all their hearts,' Robert moaned.

Suddenly Lamb stopped crying, and there was the sound of someone breathing out in a big sigh. The children turned around to see the sand fairy sitting behind them.

'Good morning,' it said. 'That wish was easy to do. Everyone wants Lamb now.'

The children realised their mistake at once, and asked if the sand fairy could take back Robert's wish and give them another one instead. The stubborn sand fairy refused and told the children to be careful what they wished for in future. Then it disappeared in a swirl of sand. The children carefully marked the spot with some stones this time.

As the children were leaving the gravel pit, a smart carriage passed by. Lady Chittenden sat inside the carriage. She was dressed from head to toe in pale lace with red ribbons, and a white fluffy dog sat on her lap. They waved to the lady and thought she would pass by but her carriage stopped.

‘What a darling baby,’ said the lady, looking at Lamb. ‘I would like to adopt him.’

‘You can’t, as he has a mother and father who love him,’ replied Anthea.

The lady opened the carriage door and jumped out. She wore some beautiful red shoes with silver buckles.

‘Can I hold him for a minute?’ she asked.

As soon as Lady Chittenden had Lamb in her arms, she jumped back into the carriage, slammed the door and shouted ‘Drive on!’

to her driver. Lamb screamed and the little dog barked. The children ran after the carriage and were able to grab hold of the back of it. As it bounced along the dusty road, the children bounced along with it.

At last the carriage stopped beside a cottage in a grand park. The children scrambled underneath it to hide. Lamb was quiet now as he had fallen asleep. The lady laid him down inside the carriage, then she got out and popped over to the cottage. The driver and the footman both sprang from their seats and bent over the sleeping Lamb.

'What a fine baby. I wish he was mine,' said the driver. 'I'll hide him in the bushes and tell the lady that his siblings took him. Then I'll come back for him afterwards.'

'No you won't,' replied the footman. 'I'm going to keep him.'

The driver hit the footman on the chin, and the footman hit the driver on the shoulder. All of a sudden a fight broke out between the two men. Cyril spotted his chance. He crawled out from under the carriage and quietly opened the carriage door. The two men were too busy fighting to notice him. He took Lamb in his arms and carried the sleeping baby along the road into a wood nearby. The other children followed,

and they all hid amongst the hazel trees and oak trees, covered by bushy ferns. They heard the angry voices of the men, followed by the angry voice of Lady Chittenden. Then, after what seemed like a long time, the carriage drove away at last.

'Well, everyone really does want Lamb now!' said Cyril. 'That sand fairy has tricked us again!'

They had a long walk home, carrying the sleeping Lamb. It was not an easy walk, as they came across many people who admired Lamb so much they wanted to take him home. They soon learnt to hide in a hedge whenever they saw someone coming.

It was very late by the time they arrived home for dinner, and Martha scolded them again.

Chapter Four

At breakfast the next morning, Robert sneakily poured some milky porridge over Lamb, so that the baby was taken away to be washed straight after breakfast. This was a naughty thing to do, but it meant that they could slip away to the gravel pit without the baby.

'I have an idea. Let's all take turns to have a wish, and I would like the first one,' said Anthea on the way to the gravel pit. She told the others that she would wish for them all to have beautiful wings. Everyone was excited by this and agreed.

Anthea told her wish to the sand fairy. The sand fairy puffed itself up, and the next moment each child felt a funny tingling in their shoulders. The sand fairy leant its head to one side and turned its snail eyes from one side to the other, then breathed out deeply.

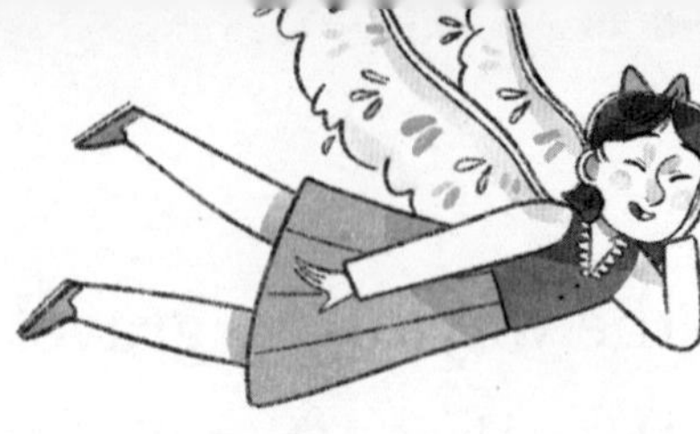

The children's wings were bigger and more beautiful than you could imagine. The feathers were soft and smooth, and they shone in many colours, like a rainbow.

Robert opened out his wings and jumped up. Slowly he began to rise in the air. The others copied him, and they, too, began to rise. It felt good to

feel the air against their faces, and they soon learnt how to fly.

They flapped their huge rainbow wings and flew for hours, with the green earth below and the blue sky above. But after a while they were tired and hungry, and their wings grew stiff.

'We are not strong enough to fly all the way home without any lunch,' said Robert.

'There's an open kitchen window,' said Cyril, pointing

to a large, open window below. He flew closer, and spotted delicious things on the table inside – custard puddings, cold chicken, bread, pies and jam! The window was high up, but the children could easily fly to it.

They emptied out their pockets to find some money to pay for the food. Then Anthea wrote a letter on a scrap of paper she also found in her pocket.

Dear kitchen owner,

We are very hungry because we have been flying all morning, and we think it is not stealing when you are starving. We are afraid to ask you for food, as you may be frightened by our wings. We will only take what we need, and hope this money will help to pay for it.

From the four of us

They wrapped the coins in the letter, then Cyril flew in through the kitchen window. He left the money and the letter, and passed some food out to Anthea and

Robert, who were waiting outside the window. Jane kept watch and was ready to whistle if anyone came near.

The top of a tall tower was the perfect spot for their little picnic, where they wouldn't be seen. They greedily tucked into chicken and bread, and washed it down with sparkling water. In the hot sunshine and with full tummies, the children soon nodded off.

As the sun disappeared and night came, the children's wings vanished. Without their huge, soft wings to keep them warm, the four wingless children shivered and woke up. They were on the top of a tower at night, miles away from home. Cyril tried to open a little door, but it was locked!

Chapter Five

'We can't stay up here all night,' wailed Jane. 'It's freezing!'

Cyril spotted a light in a window below, meaning someone was still awake. He told the others to scream when he counted to three.

'One, two, three!'

The children screamed as loudly as they could. Their screams were so loud they frightened the owls, and people heard them in their homes. One brave man called Peter opened his door and stepped out into the dark. His wife was afraid and begged him not to go. Other people came out of their homes, and they joined Peter. The children kept shouting, and the crowd followed their cries to the tower.

People were not sure who or what was up on the tower. Peter carried a lantern and led the way

up the worn, steep, dark steps. They went round and round, up and up the twisting staircase. At the top was a little door that was locked. Luckily a key was in the lock.

Peter turned the huge, stiff key and unlocked the door. They found four trembling children holding onto each other on the other side of the door. The children had sore throats from screaming so much.

'How did you get up here?' asked Peter.

'Please take us down,' croaked Jane, 'and we'll tell you anything you like. You won't believe us, but it doesn't matter.'

It wasn't easy coming down the winding, stone tower steps in the dark, and people helped the children down. Cyril came down more carefully than the others, as he had a bottle of sparkling water hidden under his coat, and had to use both hands to keep it in place. Once they were down, the children were again asked how they got to the top of the tower.

'We walked up the steps and were so tired when we reached the top that we fell asleep. When we woke, we found the door was locked, so we started screaming,' said Robert.

'You should be ashamed of yourselves for scaring everyone like that!' said Peter's wife.

As Peter's wife scolded the

children, Peter was watching Cyril, and guessed that he was hiding something.

'What are you hiding under your coat?' asked Peter.

Cyril knew it was no use hiding the bottle any more, and he pulled it out from under his coat. Everyone in the room was astonished. They guessed that the children were the thieves who had stolen the food and drink from the kitchen, and left the note.

'We took the sparkling water out of the kitchen, and some chicken and bread. We were very hungry,

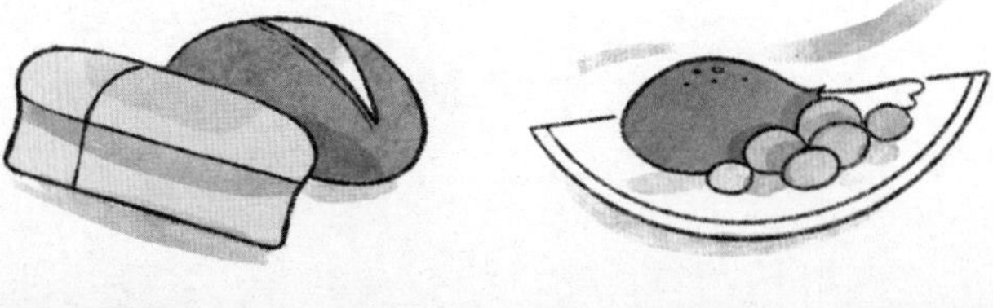

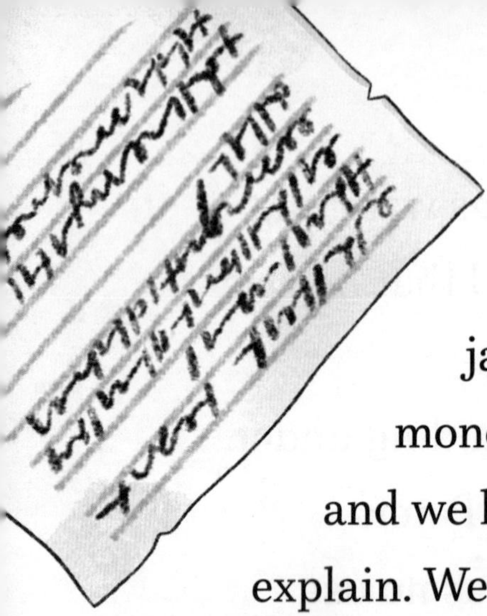

but we didn't take the pies or jam. We left some money to pay for it, and we left a letter to explain. We're very sorry. Our parents will pay a fine, but please don't send us to prison,' sobbed Cyril.

'How did you climb up to the kitchen window?' asked Peter's wife.

'I can't tell you that,' said Cyril.

The children knew the adults would not believe them if they told them they had wings and flew up to the window. The adults thought that someone older must have helped the children to steal the food.

'Did someone else make you steal the food? Are you protecting them?' asked Peter.

'Yes, but it wasn't their fault,' replied Anthea. She was thinking of the sand fairy.

The adults were happy with the children's answers, and decided that was the end of the matter. They gave the children some milk and biscuits, and then Peter took them home. Martha sent the children to bed after another telling off.

Chapter Six

The next day Martha kept the children inside as punishment. But she let Robert go out for half an hour, as he said there was something urgent he needed to do. Half an hour was all the time Robert needed to rush to the gravel pit and ask the sand fairy for his wish for the day.

Robert had no difficulty in finding the sand fairy. As it was such a hot day, for the first time,

the sand fairy was already out. It was sitting on the soft sand, stretching itself, trimming its whiskers and turning its snail's eyes round and round.

'Where are the others?' the sand fairy asked. 'I hope they haven't had an accident with those wings?'

'No, but the wings got us into trouble, just like the wishes always do,' replied Robert.

Robert told the sand fairy that the other children had been kept inside as punishment, and that he was only allowed out for half an hour.

'Wish away,' said the sand fairy, twisting itself round in the sand. But Robert couldn't wish away. He had forgotten all the things he had been thinking about, and nothing would come into his head but little things for himself, like sweets or a stamp album.

'I can't think what to wish for. I wish you could give one of the others their wish without them having to come here to ask for it. Oh, *don't*!'

It was too late! The sand fairy blew itself up to about three times its size, and then it collapsed like a pricked balloon. It breathed out deeply and leant back against the edge of the sand pool, very tired with the effort.

'It was hard, but I did it,' said the sand fairy. 'Now, run along home and tell them, before they wish for something silly before you get there!'

Robert ran home as fast as he could, but when he turned the corner that should have brought him in front of the house, he suddenly stopped. The house had disappeared! A castle now stood in its place. It was tall and wide, with battlements and long,

thin windows, and eight high towers. And instead of the garden and orchard, there were now white things dotted about like mushrooms. Robert walked closer and saw that the white things were tents, and soldiers in armour walked amongst them.

‘Oh dear,’ said Robert. ‘They have wished for a castle! It’s just like that sand fairy! I wish we had never met it!’

Robert rushed inside the castle. The others had guessed that Robert had given them his wish.

‘But you should have told us, as we may have wished for something silly,’ said Anthea.

‘Silly?’ replied Robert crossly. ‘How much sillier could you have been?’

Robert told them that soldiers were outside the castle. The children thought it would be a good idea to explore the castle and see what they could find. In a courtyard they found Martha acting strangely. She was moving her right hand backwards and forwards in the air. But the oddest thing was Lamb, who was sitting on nothing, suspended in the air, and laughing happily.

Anthea ran over to Lamb to pick him up.

'Leave him alone when he's happy,' said Martha.

'But what is he doing?' asked Anthea.

‘He’s sitting in his high chair as good as gold, watching me doing some ironing,’ replied Martha.

Martha walked across the room and poked an invisible fire with an unseen fire poker. Meanwhile, the cook walked in and put an unseen dish into an invisible oven.

‘Run along,’ said Martha. ‘We need to cook dinner.’

The children went through the first door they came to, and sat down helplessly on a wooden bench.

‘What is going on?’ said Anthea. ‘I don’t like it. I wish we’d wished for something plain, like a rocking horse or a donkey.'

'I've guessed what's going on!' beamed Cyril. 'We wished that the servants couldn't see our wishes, so of course they don't notice the castle or anything, and they are still in the house. But we can't see our house at all because we are in our wish!'

'That's all making my head swim!' said Jane.

The children climbed to the top of a tower to see what was going on outside. There were

soldiers and tents all around the castle and beyond the moat. Shivers ran down the children's backs as they saw that all the soldiers were busy cleaning or sharpening their weapons and polishing their shields. Some soldiers on horses were dragging a huge tree trunk towards the large wooden castle doors. The soldiers were getting ready to attack the castle.

Robert had an idea. He told the others to fill as many buckets

as they could with water from a deep well in the courtyard.

Suddenly, the loud, fierce sound of a trumpet rang out.

'The attack has begun,' said Robert, scared.

The children looked out over the castle walls. Soldiers were rushing about, as small as ants from where the children stood. A man stepped towards the castle.

'In the name of our trusty leader Sir Wulfric de Talbot, we order you to surrender. Do you surrender?' he bellowed.

surrender

To give up or hand over.

‘No! Never!’ bawled Robert.

The castle rattled and shook, and then there was a crash. A soldier had got inside the castle and lowered the drawbridge. This was followed by the sound of armed soldiers and horses’ hooves tramping over the bridge. Then there was the thundering thump of the tree trunk against the huge castle doors. It was getting dark inside the castle, and Jane hoped that it would soon be sunset, when the wish would vanish.

‘Hurry!’ shouted Robert. ‘Tip the water on them!’

The others followed Robert's orders and quickly poured water over the castle walls. There were groans and splashes from below as soldiers fell down.

Then, all of a sudden, it was dark. The castle seemed to whirl around and turn topsy-turvy.

Then everything disappeared. The children were safe and back in the big front bedroom of their home.

They crowded round the window. The tents and all the soldiers had gone. There was the garden, with its tangle of marigolds and roses, the spiky iron fence and the quiet road.

'Aren't you glad now that I wished for a castle?' said Cyril.

'I think so, but I wouldn't wish for it again,' replied Anthea.

'This is the first thing we've wished for that hasn't got us into trouble,' said Jane.

The bedroom door opened suddenly, and there was Martha looking cross.

'You should be ashamed of yourselves,' she said in an angry voice. 'I knew you couldn't last the day without getting into mischief. What do you mean by pouring water on people's heads when they have just stepped outside? Now off you go to bed, and try to behave better tomorrow.'

'I thought it was too good to be true!' said Cyril.

Chapter Seven

The next morning the children were struggling to think of a wish for the day. They went outside to play a pretend game of robbers and hoped that a wish would pop into their heads soon. Meanwhile, the baker's boy came along the road with some loaves in a basket.

'You there, stop!' shouted Robert, who was still playing the game.

'Your money or your life?' added Cyril cheerfully.

The baker's boy had work to do and did not want to play their game. He pushed them out of his way. Robert cheekily lassoed the baker's boy with Jane's skipping rope. He meant to loop it round the boy's shoulders, but instead it dropped to his feet and tripped him up. The baker's boy dropped his basket and beautiful fresh loaves bounced all over the dusty road. A fight broke out between Robert and the baker's boy, while the others scrambled to pick up

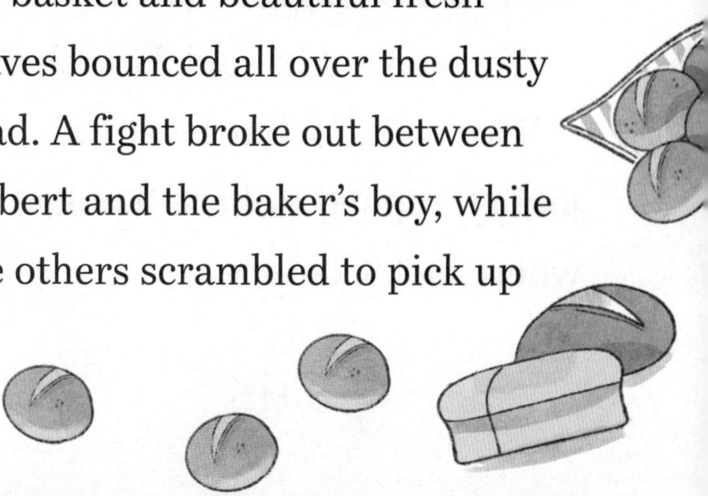

the loaves. The baker's boy was bigger than Robert and kicked him. Robert ran off towards the gravel pit, with the baker's boy chasing. With one last shove, the boy pushed Robert into the sand. He picked up his loaves, called the children silly idiots, and left.

Robert dug his hands and feet into the sand in anger.

'He thinks he can bully me just because he's bigger than me!'

'You started it,' said Jane shyly.

'I know I did, but I was only joking,' replied Robert. 'Look at where he kicked me.'

Robert showed them a large purple bruise.

'I wish I was bigger than him,' said Robert.

Robert's fingers touched something furry in the sand, and he sprang up. It was the sand fairy! And of course, the next moment Robert's wish was granted, and he was bigger than the baker's boy! Much bigger! He was the biggest person they had ever seen.

'The sand fairy has tricked us again!' said Cyril.

'What shall we do?' asked Anthea, worried.

'First, I'm going to find that baker's boy,' said Robert.

His steps were so long that he was at the bottom of the hill in no time, ready to meet the baker's boy when he returned to wait for his master's cart. He heard the boy whistling as he came along, and picked him up and set him on top of a haystack.

'Now,' Robert said. His voice was about four times its usual size, just as his body was four times its usual size. 'I'm going to teach you a lesson that it's wrong to kick boys who are smaller than you.'

Robert left the boy on the haystack. Somehow, the baker's boy later found his way down, but he had missed his master's cart and had to walk back to the bakery in the hot weather. He had learnt his lesson that it was wrong to pick on smaller boys.

When Robert returned, he met the other children in the garden. They told him how many of the servants had been talking about the fair.

'I wish we were going to the fair,' said Robert.

'You can't go anywhere that size,' replied Cyril.

'We can take Robert to the fair!' cried Jane. 'We'll ask for money to show him. Then we'll really get something out of the sand fairy at last.'

The fair was held in a meadow nearby. The children found Bill, the owner of the fair, inside the biggest tent. Robert had to crouch because the tent was not big

enough for him to stand upright in. Bill could not hold back his excitement when he saw the giant Robert. At once he agreed to pay Robert an amount for the day, and handed over a pile of coins.

'We'll fix you with some more dates when the show's over tonight. You'll be so happy with us, you'll never want to leave. Young man, your fortune will be made!' gushed Bill.

Bill knew the fair business. In a very short time, an old red and black carpet was wrapped across the tent to make a curtain to hide

Robert behind. Bill stood on a small table outside the tent and gave a speech. He invented a story and told his audience that the giant was the eldest son of the Emperor of San Francisco and the Duchess of the Fiji Islands. He ended by saying that the first twenty people who came through the tent door to see the giant would only pay three pence each. But after that, the price would go up. Even three pence was a lot, as everything else in the fair only cost one penny.

The flap of the tent was raised

and people excitedly went inside. People kept going in all afternoon, and Robert shook hands with those who wished it, and let others pull and pat him to make sure that he was real. News of the giant spread, and people arrived

in carriages and carts from near and far. The other children sat on a bench and watched and waited. They were very bored. Why had they agreed to only fifteen shillings for the day, when Bill had taken four times that already?

When Robert was at last given a break for some tea, he spoke to the other children.

'How am I to get away?' he asked, exhausted.

'Just walk out when the sun sets and you're back to your right size,' replied Cyril.

'Bill will be mad!' answered

Robert. 'No, I must be alone when the sun sets.'

Cyril went to find Bill.

'The giant *must* be left alone when the sun sets, as he's very strange at that time of day,' said Cyril firmly.

'Why, what happens?' asked Bill.

'He's not himself. Someone will get hurt if he's not alone at sunset,' replied Cyril.

'He'll be okay for the evening after that, won't he?' checked Bill.

'Oh yes. Half an hour after sunset, he'll be himself again,' said Cyril.

Bill did not want to anger the giant who was making him so much money. So, at sunset, he closed the tent for half an hour. Robert shrank back to his normal size and was able to sneak out of the tent without being spotted. The children ran all the way home, not daring to look back. They would never know how angry Bill was when he found out that he had been tricked.

Chapter Eight

The next morning Cyril snuck off to the gravel pit to ask the sand fairy for a favour.

'Can you let us have our wishes wherever we are, so we don't have to come here and disturb you?' he asked.

'It will only end in you wishing for something you don't really want, as you did with the castle,' said the sand fairy, stretching

its brown arms and yawning. 'However, if that's what you want … Goodbye.'

Cyril caught up with the other children, who had set off down the lane. They had taken Lamb with them today.

'Babies are babies for such a long time,' said Cyril angrily, as they sat on some mossy grass under a sweet chestnut tree. Cyril was cross because Lamb had played with his watch in the garden earlier, and it was now muddy and broken.

'Lamb will grow up some day,'

said Anthea, who was dreamily looking up at the blue sky between the long, straight chestnut leaves.

At that moment Lamb wriggled in Cyril's arms, and he thrust out a chubby little foot against his brother's chest. There was a crack as the glass face of a watch in Cyril's pocket broke. It was the second watch Lamb had broken that day! Cyril had borrowed the watch from his father, after Lamb had broken his.

'I wish you'd grow up!' said Cyril bitterly, putting Lamb down on the grass.

The sand fairy was true to its promise, and there, before the horrified eyes of his brothers and sisters, Lamb suddenly grew up. His face changed first: lines grew across his forehead, his eyes darkened, his mouth grew longer and thinner – and most terrible of all, a little dark moustache appeared on his top lip. Then little Lamb was all grown up.

At that moment a lady passed by. She was pushing a bicycle and looked upset.

'Can I help you?' asked grown-up Lamb politely.

The lady told Lamb that her bicycle had

a puncture. Lamb bent down to look at it. He talked to her in a very grown-up way, and soon mended her bicycle.

'I will ride with you as far as the crossroads, as it's getting late,' he said.

'Don't let him,' said Anthea to the lady.

'Don't be silly, little girl,' said Lamb.

'He doesn't know who he is,' the now reckless Anthea went on. 'He's something very different to what you think he is.'

'What do you mean?' asked the

lady, who was looking worried now.

'We're his big brothers and sisters,' Jane added.

'We've got to take care of him. And we must get him home before sunset. He's sort of under a spell,' said Cyril.

Robert and Cyril each held onto one of Lamb's legs to stop him leaving with the lady. The frightened lady quickly rode away.

'You are all acting so strangely that I will take you home now. But we will talk about your behaviour in the morning,' grown-up Lamb said to his brothers and sisters.

The sun was about to set when they arrived home. The four older children would have liked to have waited until the sun had set and Lamb was once again their baby

brother, but the grown-up Lamb wanted to hurry home. They were met by Martha in the garden.

Remember, Martha could not see the wishes granted by the sand fairy, so she saw the children returning with the baby Lamb.

'Come to Martha, my precious poppet,' Martha said, as she picked up the shocked grown-up Lamb and turned to carry him into the house.

Luckily the sun set as they reached the doorstep, and Martha now carried the darling, sleepy, baby Lamb.

Chapter Nine

The children were wondering what to wish for at breakfast the next morning, when a letter arrived from their mother. It said

that their grandmother was better, and that their mother would arrive later that day.

'Let's make a wish for Mother today,' said Cyril.

'I wonder what she would like?' said Jane.

They were interrupted by Martha, who had heard some bad news. Burglars had stolen Lady Chittenden's diamond jewellery, including necklaces, bracelets and tiaras. The children remembered that it was Lady Chittenden who had tried to take Lamb away.

'I don't see why she should have so many diamonds,' said Anthea, when Martha left the room. 'I did not like her much. Mother doesn't have any diamonds.'

'I wish Mother could have all Lady Chittenden's lovely jewellery in her room when she comes home,' said Jane dreamily.

The others gazed at Jane in horror.

'Well, she will now, as you've just wished for it!' said Robert.

As soon as their mother arrived, she went upstairs to her room. The children followed her, dreading what she would find there.

First, Mother took off her flowery bonnet, and then she went to the dressing table to comb her pretty hair. A green leather case lay on her dressing table. Mother opened it and found a ring with a large pearl surrounded by little diamonds.

'Oh, how lovely,' cried Mother as she fitted the ring on her finger.

'Wherever did this come from?'

'I don't know,' said each of the children nervously.

'Father must have told Martha to put it here,' said Mother. 'I'll run down and ask her.'

But when Martha was asked, she knew nothing of the ring, and neither did any of the other servants. Mother returned to her bedroom and opened her dressing table drawer. She found a long case containing a priceless diamond necklace. In the wardrobe she found a

tiara and many brooches. The rest of Lady Chittenden's jewellery turned up over the next half an hour, all over Mother's room. Jane began to cry.

'Jane, what do you know about this?' asked Mother.

'We found a fairy,' replied Jane truthfully.

'Don't be silly!' said her mother, raising her eyebrows.

Cyril told their mother how thieves had stolen Lady Chittenden's jewellery last night.

He wondered if the jewels belonged to her. Mother went downstairs and asked Martha if any strangers had been in her room. Only Beale, the window cleaner, had been in to Mother's room recently to clean the windows.

The children felt terrible that an innocent man would be accused of robbery all because of Jane's silly wish. But neither their mother nor anyone else would believe them about the sand fairy.

'I will take the cart to Rochester and report this to the police,' said Mother.

The children begged their mother not to go, but their mother was stubborn and would not listen.

The children's only hope of fixing things was to beg the sand fairy to undo the wish. So they ran off to the gravel pit. They found the sand fairy sunbathing in a golden, sandy hollow and washing its whiskers happily in the glowing afternoon sun.

The moment it saw them, it whisked round and began to burrow back underground. But Anthea was too quick for it and caught it by its furry shoulders. She held onto it gently but firmly.

'Let go of me,' said the sand fairy grumpily. 'I guess you want another wish.'

'Do you hate giving wishes?' asked Anthea.

'Of course I do. It's such hard work to puff myself up with other people's wishes, and I almost burst giving them,' replied the sand fairy.

'If you'll do what we ask today, we'll never ask you for another wish as long as we live,' said Anthea kindly.

The children had a long list of wishes that day, as many things needed fixing. Anthea asked for Lady Chittenden's jewels to be returned, for their mother not to see the police, and for everyone to forget about the diamonds and Beale the window cleaner.

When the sand fairy had finished, it asked Anthea to make it a wish, as it could not make a wish for itself.

'Can you wish that none of you will ever be able to tell anyone about *me*?'

If everyone started asking it for wishes, not only would it tire the sand fairy out, but the whole world would be in a muddle.

When Anthea had done that,

the sand fairy asked the children if there was anything else.

'No,' Jane replied. 'Thank you so much for all you've done for us, and I hope you'll have a good long sleep, and I hope we shall see you again one day.'

'Is that a wish?' the sand fairy said in a weak voice.

'Yes please,' all the children answered.

Then, for the last time in this story, they saw the sand fairy puff itself up, then breathe out deeply.

It nodded to them, blinked its long snail's eyes, burrowed into the sand and disappeared.

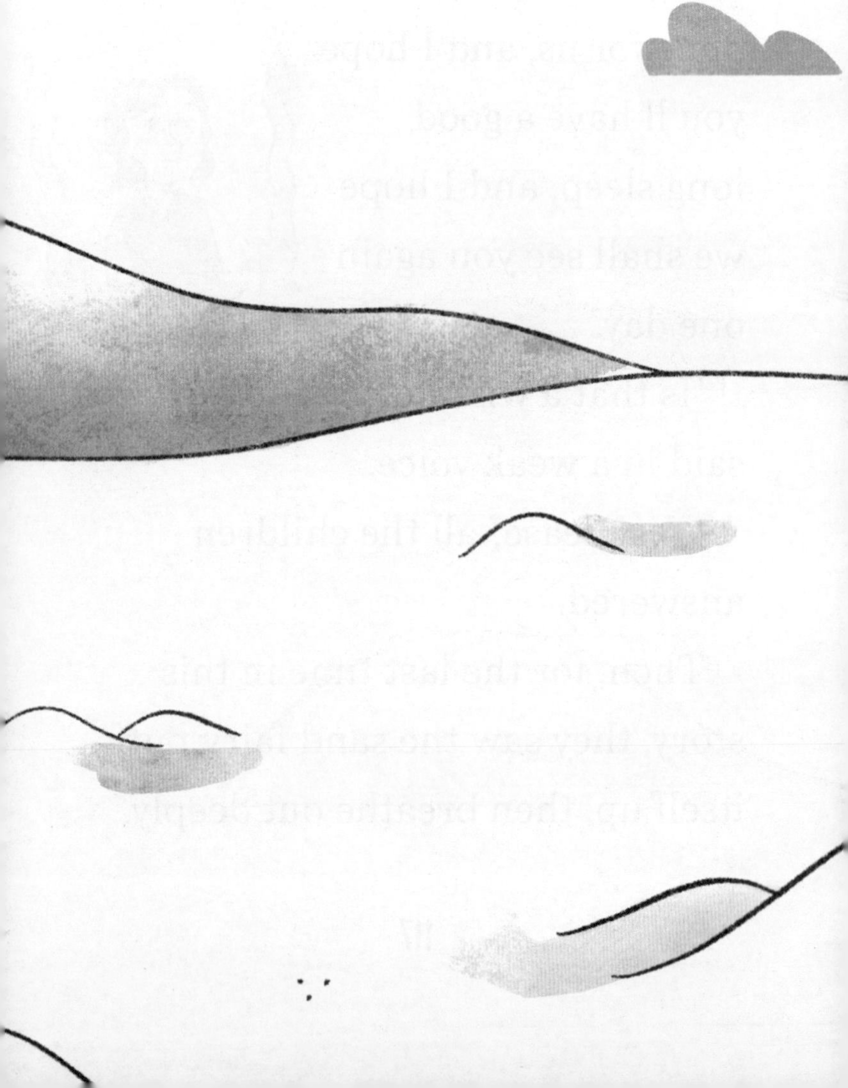

Edith Nesbit

Edith Nesbit was born in London in 1858. Her family travelled throughout much of Europe when Nesbit was young, in an attempt to cure her sister's illness. They finally settled in Kent, England. Nesbit had a clear talent for poetry that was spotted in her teens. Her further success as a writer meant she dedicated most of her life to writing for children and adults. *Five Children and It* was first published in 1902.